★ Larry Schwarz ★★★ Illustrated by Kelly Denato ★

LITTLE, BROWN AND COMPANY
New York ~ Boston

TO KAREN MILLER, FOR MAKING THIS BOOK HAPPEN, AND MY MOTHER,
FOR MAKING ME HAPPEN. —L.S.

FOR MY MOM. —K.D.

Text and Illustrations copyright © 2006 by Kanonen & Bestreichen, Inc.
All rights reserved.
Little, Brown and Company   Time Warner Book Group   1271 Avenue of the Americas, New York, NY 10020
Visit our Web site at www.lb-kids.com
First Edition: June 2006
Schwarz, Larry.   Ellen's 11-star spectacular super deluxe hotel / by Larry Schwarz ; illustrated by Kelly Denato.— 1st ed.
p. cm.   Summary: A little girl with a big imagination solves the mystery of Princess Zara and the missing crown jewels of Sedelbania.
ISBN 0-316-86902-3 [1. Hotels, motels, etc.—Fiction. 2. Mystery and detective stories. 3. Humorous stories.]
I. Denato, Kelly, ill. II. Title. III. Title: Ellen's eleven-star spectacular super deluxe hotel.
PZ7.S4116El 2005   [E]—dc22   2004005307
10 9 8 7 6 5 4 3 2 1
TWP   Printed in Singapore

Hi. My name is Ellen, and this is my hotel.

Actually, it belongs to my parents.

It's an 11-star spectacular luxury hotel with all sorts of deluxe accommodations.

Well, actually, it's a motel outside Carson City, Nevada.

We have a swimming pool, a jungle gym, and a really neat
ice-making machine.

I have all these cool friends who come around and play after school, and we have a lot of fun.

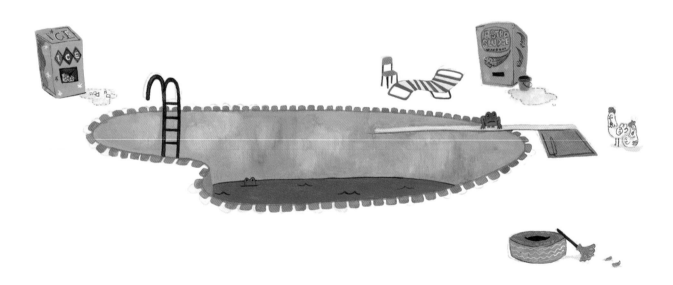

Well, actually, there aren't too many kids—or anyone, really—
for miles around.

All sorts of famous movie stars, musicians, astronauts, and artists stay at our hotel.

Well, actually, the customers aren't that fancy.

But I do have this 2200 XYS dual-traction, all-season radial tire and this deluxe guaranteed-sneeze-proof Emu feather duster. *Achoo!*

And I do get to go on these great adventures.

One day, I was feeding ambrosia to my Siberian silver-scaled lizard....

Actually, I was tossing Astro Sludge Jelly and Lard Pies that I got from the vending machine into my tire...

When I saw Princess Zara running through the palace courtyard. Someone had stolen the crown jewels of Sedelbania!

Well, actually, it was Mrs. Sedelberg in room 609 screaming that all her luggage had been stolen.

Luckily for the princess and the good citizens of Sedelbania, a world-renowned detective happened to be passing through at that very moment.

Well, actually, it was me! I quickly took the case.

Using my ultra-supersonic telescopic sonar microphone, I interviewed Victor and Vespa, two international film stars who were staying at the hotel while attending the Sedelbania Film Festival.

Well, actually, I interviewed Cooter and Connie. They're the Emerald Acres' handyman and maid. But they had been too busy watching an in-room movie and hadn't seen a thing.

I examined the princess's throne room for clues, using my satellite downlink laser imager.

Who could have stolen the crown jewels? Was it Princess Zara's ex-boyfriend, the suave and dashing Count Alfred? Could it be the mysterious one-armed stranger?

Or could it be the princess's jealous sisters, Morgan, Taryn, and Keaton?

Actually, Mrs. Sedelberg had gone into Room 606 instead of 609.

The number on her door was upside down! The princess's crown jewels had been safe all along in the *real* room 609.

The princess rewarded the famous detective by giving her a bag of treasure and an all-expenses paid vacation to a tropical island resort.

Well, actually…